The Little Red Hen

A Folk Tale

Adapted by:
Margaret Ann Hughes
Ken Forsse

Illustrated by:
Russell Hicks
Douglas McCarthy
Theresa Mazurek
Allyn Conley-Gorniak
Julie Ann Armstrong

This Book Belongs To:

Use this symbol to match book and cassette.

Once upon a time there was a big yellow house in the country. In the house there lived a dog, a cat, a mouse and a little red hen. Well, the dog, the cat, and the mouse just rested all day long, while the little red hen worked and worked and worked.

The dog was named Benjamin. He was an old white dog with dark brown spots, long floppy ears, great big paws, and a sloppy wet nose. Benjamin was no help around the house at all.

He seemed to have lots of excuses for not doing any work.

Now Benjamin's favorite place was a warm sunny spot on the front porch. There he'd sleep in the morning. Then in the afternoon, he'd move himself to the sunny spot on the back porch. And at night he'd move into the living room by the fire.

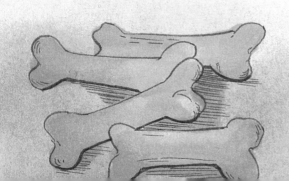

The cat was named Prissy. She was a yellow Persian cat with long, soft fur. All day long, if she wasn't sleeping, she would wash her fur and fluff it out just as big and puffy as could be. Prissy had royal ancestors, you see. Prissy had lots of reasons for not working…so she never did.

As she rested on her satin pillow, Prissy thought only the most pleasant of thoughts. She would never bother to chase a mouse, which was fortunate for Max, since he was… a mouse.

Well, Max was a little gray mouse with pink ears…and, like Benjamin and Prissy, had lots of excuses for not working. He preferred to curl up inside the couch.

Now everyone knows that there are things around the house that need to be done each day, like cooking, cleaning, washing and gardening. But with the dog, the cat, and the mouse sleeping all day, the only one left to do all the work was the little red hen. Her name was Emma.

Emma was a cute little red hen. She wore a blue checked apron as she went about her many chores. And Emma was a smart little hen. She knew that there were things that had to be done, and she worked hard, but she really needed help. She tried to get the others to help. She asked Benjamin...

...she asked Prissy...

...and she asked Max.

No one would help her with the work, so Emma felt very sad.

Emma tried her best, but she just couldn't get anyone to help. They all had excuses. But the fact is that they were lazy. Then one day, while weeding the garden, Emma found some grains of wheat.

Emma took the wheat into the house. She asked for help to plant it.

As usual, the dog, the cat and the mouse refused to help. So the little red hen took her shovel, and her hoe, and planted the wheat in a special place in the garden. And every day she asked for help to water the wheat.

With no one to help, the little red hen took care
of the wheat by herself, and it grew, and it grew,
and it grew. When the wheat was tall enough,
Emma decided it was time to harvest it.
And so she asked for help.

Again, Emma had to do the work all by herself.
She took a scythe and cut down all the wheat.
Then she placed it on top of a large blanket and
beat it until all the wheat kernels separated from
the stalks. Then it was time to grind the wheat
into flour, and again, she asked the dog, the cat,
and the mouse for help.

Because no one would help her, Emma
went to the mill alone to grind the
wheat into nice fine brown flour.

Then she hurried back to
the big yellow house
to bake some bread.

Emma mixed the batter for bread, using flour and eggs and milk. As she kneaded the dough, she hummed and smiled. Emma seemed especially happy! When the dough had risen, she put it in a pan, and then put the pan into the oven. Before long, the whole house began to smell of baking bread. Benjamin's extra sensitive nose smelled the bread first.

The cat and the mouse also woke up as their noses filled with the wonderful smell of homemade wheat bread.

The dog, the cat and the mouse eagerly gathered around the warm bread. Although they hadn't done a thing to help, they wanted to help eat it.

Since Emma had done the work all by herself, she ate the bread all by herself, smiling just a little inside, as the others stood by watching. She knew they had just learned a very valuable lesson.

From that day on,
the little red hen
never had any trouble getting help with the work
around the house. The cat was helpful…

…and the mouse stopped sleeping all the time…

…and the dog was always ready to lend a hand.

While everyone helped, the little red hen baked an apple pie. All of the housework and the yardwork was done so quickly. And when everything was finished, everyone ate the apple pie and enjoyed "the fruits of their labor!"

 *nd they all lived happily ever after.*